For Vincent

First American edition published in 2010
by Boxer Books Limited.

First published in Great Britain in 2010
by Boxer Books Limited.
www.boxerbooks.com

Text and illustrations copyright © 2010 Britta Teckentrup

The rights of Britta Teckentrup to be identified as the author and
illustrator of this work have been asserted by her
in accordance with the Copyright, Designs and Patents Act, 1988.

All rights reserved, including the right of reproduction in whole or in part in any form.
Library of Congress Cataloging-in-Publication Data available.

The illustrations were prepared using hand printed paper and digital collage.
The text is set in Adobe Garamond Pro regular.

ISBN 978-1-907152-33-7

1 3 5 7 9 10 8 6 4 2

Printed in China

All of our papers are sourced from managed forests and renewable resources.

LITTLE WOLF'S
SONG

Britta Teckentrup

Boxer Books

Little Wolf lived high up in the mountains.
Every night his family howled, as all wolves
do. Mommy had a warm, motherly howl.
Daddy had a strong, deep howl.
His brothers had a happy, yappy howl,
and his sister's howl was sweet and lovely.
Together they sang a beautiful song.
But Little Wolf had no howl at all.

All he could manage was a little squeak.

His brothers and sister teased Little Wolf.

"A wolf who can't howl isn't a real wolf at all!"

"Let's call him Squeaky!" they said, laughing.
This made Little Wolf very sad.

"Don't listen to them," said Daddy.

Mommy said, "You just have to give it time.
One day, when the time is right, you will
be able to howl."

So Little Wolf tried not to worry.
While his brothers and sister played,
he wandered off alone, watching the
birds and listening to their songs.

One afternoon, Little Wolf was
chasing snowflakes.

He ran up and down and all around,
trying to catch as many as he could.

The fresh, cold snow was so delicious!

Up the hill he ran, farther and farther, until . . .

Little Wolf didn't know where he was.

He had never been this far away from home.

He looked around.

Nothing looked familiar.

Little Wolf ran back and forth,

trying to find the way home.

But he was lost!

Soon it grew dark, and Little Wolf
was frightened. But when a perfect
full moon rose in the sky,
everything started to glisten.

The only thing Little Wolf could hear
was the gentle sound of snow falling.
He looked up at the big yellow moon,
and the time felt just right.

HOOOOOOOOWL!

The sound of the most beautiful howl traveled through the night sky.

Suddenly a deep voice behind him said,

"Here you are, Little Wolf."

Little Wolf knew this voice well.

"Daddy, Daddy! Did you hear me?"

"Yes, Little Wolf. That's how I found you."

"Let's go home and tell your mother!"
said Daddy. "She must be worried."
Little Wolf scampered ahead.
"Come on, Daddy, hurry!" he said.

Little Wolf's family was very proud.
His sister made him tell his story over
and over again, and his brothers said,
"Come on! Let's all practice howling together!"
Little Wolf led the others.

Now, whenever there is a full moon,
Little Wolf and his father
go up to that magical place.

And you can hear them
howling at the moon together . . .
the most beautiful song you
have ever heard.